Arthur A. Levine pictures by Susan Guevara

THE BOARDWALK PRINCESS

TAMBOURINE BOOKS NEW YORK

Text copyright © 1993 by Arthur A. Levine
Illustrations copyright © 1993 by Susan Guevara

Tambourine Books, a division of William Morrow & Company, Inc.,
1350 Avenue of the Americas, New York, New York 10019.
Printed in the United States of America.
The full-color illustrations were created with
pencil, acrylic, and gouache on jessoed paper.

The Boardwalk Princess is inspired by Jacob and Wilhelm Grimm's
Brüderchen und Schwesterchen (Brother and Sister).

Library of Congress Cataloging in Publication Data

Levine, Arthur A., 1962-The boardwalk princess/by Arthur Levine:
illustrated by Susan Guevara. — 1st ed. p. cm.
Summary: In this modernized version of the Grimm fairy tale
"Brother and Sister," Brooklyn siblings Myron and Sadie are victims
of a spell cast by a greedy witch.
[1. Fairy tales.   2. Folklore–Germany.]   I. Guevara, Susan, ill.   II. Title.
PZ8.L4789   Bo 1993   398.21–dc20 [E] 92-8081 CIP AC
ISBN 0-688-10306-5.—ISBN 0-688-10307-3 (lib. bdg.)

10 9 8 7 6 5 4 3 2 1
FIRST EDITION

For Susan Cohen, Agenting Goddess, who sent
me to Brooklyn in the first place

A.L.

It's for you, Pop

S.G.

Once upon a time, in a strange land called Brooklyn, a
brother and sister named Myron and Sadie made the most
fabulous and beautiful clothing you could imagine.

Material actually spoke to Sadie. If she put her ear to a calico it might whisper, "Use a patch of me." Or a corduroy might ask, "Wouldn't I make an elegant stripe?" And the fabric was always, magically, right.

In the market Myron could smell quality two stalls away. Fabric he turned down shrank and bled. And fabric he bought? Magic.

But with all this wondrous talent, were they a happy
pair? No. Orphaned at a young age, Myron and Sadie
were adopted by an evil old witch who knew a good thing
when she saw it.

All day and all night the witch kept Myron and Sadie
slaving away so she could sell their creations in her
fashionable boutique. The chic sought her out. The
famous fawned. And her money jars overflowed. Never
mind that she ran a sweatshop.

Finally Myron and Sadie could take it no more. In the middle of the night they packed up their favorite bolts and spools. And in the morning they fled.

Too bad nothing was lost on that old witch. She followed them, clutching an evil potion and snarling, "I'll teach those ingrates to run away."

Soon Myron and Sadie passed a park with trees and
benches and a round stone fountain. Myron leaned over
to drink, but while his head was turned the witch emptied
several drops of her potion into the water.

Suddenly Sadie heard the fountain gurgling: "Drink of
me, drink of me, fill a cool cup, then from the water a cat
shall look up!" And in the clear stream the shape of an
angry cat hissed and snapped.

"No!" Sadie shouted, "Stop!"

Well, thirsty as he was, Myron had always listened
when things spoke to Sadie. So he stood up with a sigh
and on they went.

After a while they came to a courtyard with a tiled pond in the center. Myron gratefully cupped his hands to drink.

At that moment a tinkling voice called to Sadie, "Drink of me, drink of me, fill a cool cup, then from the water a dog shall look up!" And in the spray a misty dog-shape stood, its fangs dripping. Sadie dashed over and pulled Myron away.

So Myron left with his throat parched once again and the two orphans stumbled deeper into the city. Finally they came across a fire hydrant that *someone* had just opened.

This time Myron couldn't resist and Sadie couldn't stop him. He drank as if he'd been in the desert.

Suddenly the air grew brighter. Just as Myron wiped his dripping mouth there was a flash and a pop, and in the boy's place stood a mouse.

"Now let's see how you do all alone without your precious Myron," laughed the old witch. And then she was gone.

But Sadie was not all alone. She had her bags full of fabric. And she still had Myron, even if he was a mouse.

So they walked and walked until they reached a boardwalk next to the ocean. Then Sadie took out some bolts of cloth, listened carefully, and started making a tent. Myron-the-mouse sniffed out the best pieces to use, and brought her new material from nearby. Before long they had a magnificent shelter of heavy printed wool and umbrella handles, trimmed with golden thread and colorful telegraph wire.

For a long time Myron and Sadie lived quietly by the sea, making tiny coats for cold-looking pigeons and scarves for squirrels who brought them nuts.

Then one day a crowd of people showed up not far from the marvelous tent. They all stood around one tall, handsome man, asking questions.

"And the Ferris Wheel will be over there, and the Giant Roller Coaster here," he was saying in a satiny voice. Myron's nose twitched wildly—he smelled quality clothing like he never had before. So who could blame him—he had to get a closer whiff.

Suddenly a big, black dog spotted him and broke away from the tall, handsome man. Myron ran for his life, with the entire crowd yelling and thundering along the wooden boards a few steps behind.

The dog's breath was hot on his fur when Myron jumped. And he jumped like no mouse you've ever seen— high, high in the air, so that Sadie had to stretch to catch him. Then she settled him gently into her skirt pocket.

This stopped the crowd cold.

"What have we here?" asked the tall man, finally.

"I'm an orphan," said Sadie.

"And a rather natty dresser as well," said the Real Estate Tycoon. For that's who the handsome man was. The reporters closed in and crowded around the tent, admiring Sadie and Myron's handiwork. "If you'd rather live inside, you're welcome to come with me," said the Tycoon. "That is, you and your, er, mouse, of course." And so they packed up the tent and drove off to his mansion.

Many years passed, and the Tycoon helped Sadie become a famous clothing designer. Together they were the toast of the town. And the two fell deeply in love.

Soon wedding announcements were sent to anyone who was anybody. Things would have been perfect, if only Myron weren't a mouse.

Word eventually reached the stoop of the old hag. She was last year's news now. Unstylish. A has-been. And her business had fallen apart.

"I'll get even!" she vowed. And she hatched a terrible plan.

On the eve of the wedding, Sadie's maid took ill and a poorly dressed one took her place. "I'll have to make you a new uniform," Sadie offered as the maid drew her bath. The maid kept silent as she led Sadie along. "You know, you look awfully familiar . . ." said Sadie, and just then she realized who it was. But it was too late. The hag had her by both arms and was dragging her toward the sizzling, foul waters in the tub.

But Myron, who had such a nose for value, could also smell evil a mile away. He squeezed under the door and leaped at the hag, crashing into the tub with her, whiskers and tail.

There was a loud bang and an explosion of suds. When everything settled, the old hag was gone and Myron had been transformed.

The next day the wedding took place as planned, with a real live best *man* instead of a best mouse. The Tycoon was as delighted as Sadie herself.

And the wedding dress?
Magic!